CW00970747

This book
belongs to

....

for Zoë

SMALL HOUSE IN WINTER

Stella Blackstone

Illustrated by Prue Berthon

BAREFOOT BEGINNERS
BATH

Small house in winter,
Rosie comes to stay
with her Granny and her Grandpa
for a night and a day.

Granny makes hot chocolate,
Rosie climbs the stairs
in her dressing-gown and slippers;
she dreams of polar bears.

Small house at night-time;
the fire spits and burns;
mice scamper through the eaves,
Jack Frost returns.

Stars glisten in the sky,
trees prickly white,
foxes prowl around the house,
Jack Frost bites.

Small house at daybreak,
dogs stir and bark;
Grandpa wakes to wash and shave,
Rosie's room is dark.

Cold creeps through the floor-boards,
windows are shut tight;
Rosie peeps outside and gasps –
snow falls, thick and white.

Small house in the morning,
Grandpa shovels snow;
Rosie builds a snowman,
face and fingers glow.

Granny breaks the thick, hard ice
in the hen-house tray;
Grandpa fetches Marigold
clover-scented hay.

Small house at midday,
Granny starts to bake;
Rosie wants fresh scones for tea,
Grandpa wants some cake.

Marigold is lonely;
she neighs across the yard,
Rosie strokes her on the nose,
snow crisp and hard.

Small house in the afternoon,
Grandpa splices wood;
Granny starts to tell the tale
of Red Riding Hood.

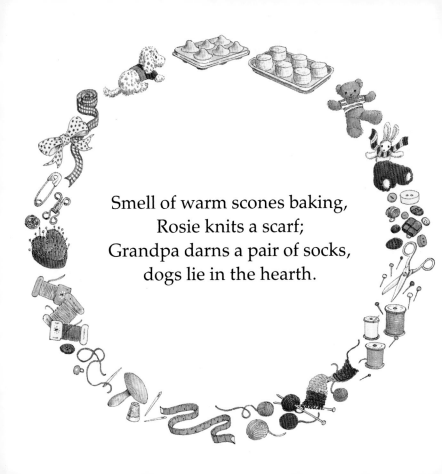

Smell of warm scones baking,
Rosie knits a scarf;
Grandpa darns a pair of socks,
dogs lie in the hearth.

Granny draws the curtains
and calls 'Tea, everyone!'
Rosie fetches cups and plates
for scones and milk and buns.

Small house in the evening,
Rosie says goodbye;
'We'll see you in the springtime!'
Granny and Grandpa cry.

BAREFOOT BEGINNERS

an imprint of

Barefoot Books Ltd
PO Box 95
Kingswood
Bristol BS15 5BH

This book has been printed on 100% acid-free paper

Text copyright © 1997 by Stella Blackstone

Illustrations copyright © 1997 by Prue Berthon

First published in Great Britain in 1997 by Barefoot Books Ltd

Printed in Hong Kong by South Seas International

ISBN: 1 898000 57 3

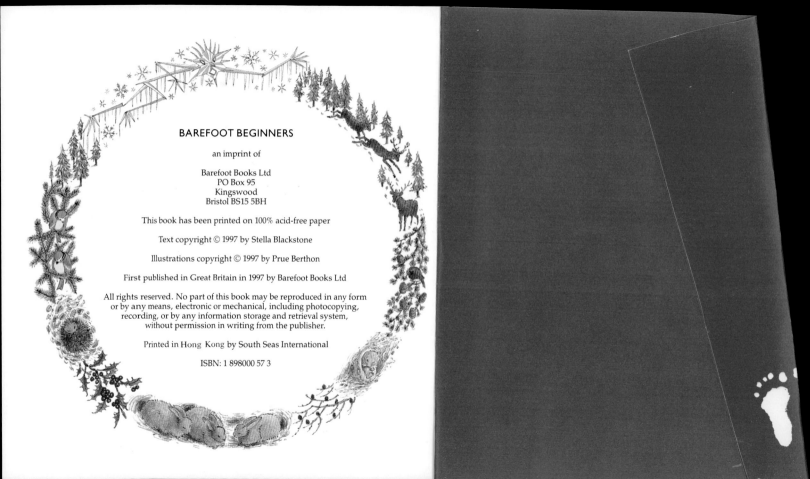